To Weston, Bennett, and Cooper — Three tough truckers! — CRS

To Bob, for steering me in the right direction. — RG

To Patti Ann, Celia, and Doan, who make all my books better. — HL

Text copyright © 2019 by Corey Rosen Schwartz and Rebecca J. Gomez · Illustrations copyright © 2019 by Hilary Leung

Library of Congress Cataloging-in-Publication Data · Names: Schwartz, Corey Rosen, author. | Gomez, Rebecca J., author. | Leung, Hilary, illustrator. · Title: Two tough trucks / by Corey Rosen Schwartz and Rebecca J. Gomez ; illustrated by Hilary Leung. · Description: First edition. | New York : Orchard Books, 2019. | Summary: Told in rhyming text, two trucks, Mack and Rig, are paired up on their first day of class--Mack is a hotshot, all speed and power, and Rig is more cautious, but on the obstacle course they learn that their separate skills can work well together. · Identifiers: LCCN 2018047089 (print) | LCCN 2018057492 (ebook) | ISBN 9781338498448 (E-Book) | ISBN 9781338236545 (jacketed hardcover) · Subjects: LCSH: Trucks--Juvenile fiction. | Friendship--Juvenile fiction. | Stories in rhyme. | CYAC: Stories in rhyme. | Trucks--Fiction. | Friendship--Fiction. | LCGFT: Stories in rhyme. Classification: LCC PZ8.3.S38927 (ebook) | LCC PZ8.3.S38927 Tw 2019 (print) | DDC [E]--dc23 · LC record available at https://catalog.loc.gov/vwebv/searchBrowse?editSearchId=E

ISBN 978-1-338-23654-5

10 9 8 7 6 5 4 3 2 1   19 20 21 22 23

Printed in China   38 · First edition, September 2019

The text type was set in Hank BT. · The display type was set in Luckiest Guy.

Book design by Doan Buu

TWO TOUGH TRUCKS

by **COREY ROSEN SCHWARTZ** and **REBECCA J. GOMEZ**

illustrated by **HILARY LEUNG**

Orchard Books
New York
An Imprint of Scholastic Inc.

One Mack, revved up and ready to go.

One Rig, a wreck, unsteady and slow.

Two trucks off to school for their first day of class.
One riding the brakes. One hitting the gas.

VROOM! ZOOM!

A beep-beep goodbye.

A Rig holding back, a Mack saying "Hi!"

Miss Rhodes said, "Good morning.
Let's head to the track."
She put them in pairs,
matching Rig up with Mack.

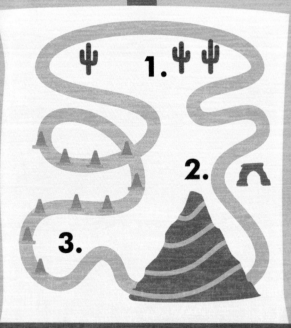

"Each team will attempt every task on this list."

"The circuit!
Let's do this."

1. 2. 3.

"Watch out
for the twist!"

VROOM! ZOOM!

A wobble and whir.

A shaky blue blob and a speedy red blur.

One Mack,
one Rig,
one very sharp turn.

"Let's roar it and floor it!
Burn, baby, burn!"

"Oh no! Hit the brakes!"

"We won't make it!" Rig cried.

But Mack sped ahead.
"Just hug the inside!"

VROOM! ZOOM!

A swish and a swerve.

Rig skidded out, but Mack aced the curve.

Miss Rhodes blew her horn, then she ran the next drill.
"Practice downshifting to get up that hill!"

They moved up the slope with a shift and a grind.

"This hill is too easy."

"Don't leave me behind!"

VROOM! ZOOM!

Their truck engines straining.
A Rig who was stalling,
a Mack who kept gaining.

One Mack
reached the crest.
"I knew I was fast."

One Rig
did his best,
but finished dead last.

"Good grief," grumbled Mack. "My partner's a drag."

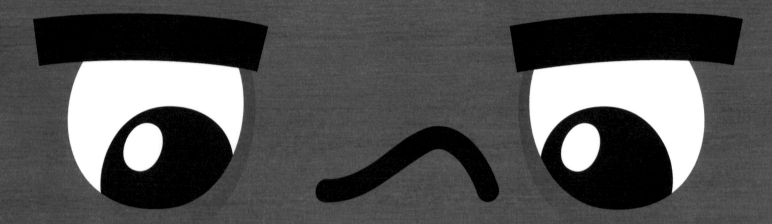

"That hotshot," said Rig. "He sure loves to brag!"

VROOM! FUME!

They vented and fussed.

A Mack making tracks, a Rig in the dust.

"It's time to go backward."

The trucks got in gear.
They all checked their mirrors
and struggled to steer.

They veered and corrected,
they turned and reversed.
Rig had good instincts,
but Mack was . . .

the worst!

VROOM! ZOOM!

A whoosh and a whack.

A confident Rig and a blundering Mack.

"I nailed it!" said Rig as he finished the course.

He turned just as Mack
hit a cone at full force.

Mack idled his engine.

"I quit. I can't do it."

"Steer left to go right.
I'll help guide you through it."

DONUTS

VROOM! ZOOM!

They backtracked and bumped.
A Mack making progress,
a Rig feeling pumped!

One Mack, one Rig,
two trucks side by side,
weaving past cones.

"We did it!" they cried.

"You really stuck by me."

"You needed me, Mack."

"Let's head back *together* to tackle that track!"

VROOM! ZOOM!

They zipped around bends.
Two *tough* trucks . . . now the fastest of friends.